My Family

My Family Celebrates

By Sophie Geister-Jones

www.littlebluehousebooks.com

Little Blue House is distributed by North Star Editions:
sales@northstareditions.com | 888-417-0195

Produced for Little Blue House by Red Line Editorial.

Photographs ©: coscaron/iStockphoto, cover; Jack Frog/Shutterstock Images, 4; xavierarnau/iStockphoto, 7, 24 (bottom right); PeopleImages/iStockphoto, 8–9; LumiNola/iStockphoto, 11; Yakobchuk Viacheslav/Shutterstock Images, 12; kirin_photo/iStockphoto, 15; MillefloreImages/iStockphoto, 16; New Africa/Shutterstock Images, 19; fstop123/iStockphoto, 21; martin-dm/iStockphoto, 23; JohnGollop/iStockphoto, 24 (top left); OnlyZoia/Shutterstock Images, 24 (top right); bluestocking/iStockphoto, 24 (bottom left)

Library of Congress Control Number: 2019908244

ISBN
978-1-64619-035-5 (hardcover)
978-1-64619-074-4 (paperback)
978-1-64619-113-0 (ebook pdf)
978-1-64619-152-9 (hosted ebook)

Printed in the United States of America
Mankato, MN
012020

About the Author

Sophie Geister-Jones likes reading, spending time with her family, and eating cheese. She lives in Minnesota.

Table of Contents

Family Celebrations

My family likes
to celebrate.
We meet at the park
and have a party.

My family celebrates Mother's Day. We give flowers to our mom. We love her very much.

flowers
mom

My family celebrates Father's Day. We play video games with our dad. We love him very much.

dad

My family likes to celebrate birthdays. We blow out candles and eat cake.

cake

Winter Celebrations

My family celebrates the New Year.

We stay up late and make noise.

My family celebrates Valentine's Day. We make cards. We celebrate our love.

card

Happy May Day!

Spring Celebrations

My family celebrates May Day.

It is on the first day of May.

We make baskets and fill them with flowers.

My family celebrates
Arbor Day.
We plant trees in
our neighborhood.

VOLUNTEER

My family celebrates
Earth Day.
We pick up trash outside.

My family celebrates many things. We always celebrate by spending time together.

Glossary

basket

card

candles

flowers

Index